FOR SWEETIE BERRY,
MY FRIEND AND COLLABORATOR,
WHO DOES SO MUCH TO MAKE IT OKAY FOR SO MANY.
—C.D.

TO MY SISTER, ELENA.
—J.L.

Text copyright © 2022 Crescent Dragonwagon
Illustrations copyright © 2022 Jessica Love

Book design by Melissa Nelson Greenberg

Published in 2022 by CAMERON + COMPANY, a division of ABRAMS.
All rights reserved. No portion of this book may be reproduced,
stored in a retrieval system, or transmitted in any form or by any means,
mechanical, electronic, photocopying, recording, or otherwise,
without written permission from the publisher.

Library of Congress Cataloging-in-Publication Data available.
ISBN: 978-1-951836-50-4

Printed in China

10 9 8 7 6 5 4 3 2 1

CAMERON KIDS is an imprint of CAMERON + COMPANY

CAMERON + COMPANY
Petaluma, California
www.cameronbooks.com

WILL IT BE OKAY?

by Crescent Dragonwagon
art by Jessica Love

cameron kids

"Will it be okay?"

"Yes, it will."

"But what if there is thunder and lightning?"

"You sit at your window
and watch the rain beating down
over the houses and streets
in the dark night.
You see how special it is,
because the lightning
shows the rainy sky and
countryside and all the city.

"You pay attention,
because the loud thunder
is calling you, saying:
Look, look!
The world is receiving
a deep long drink!"

"But what if there is snow, lots and lots of snow?"

"You put on your red leggings, and your orange boots,
and your pink coat, and your plaid scarf,
and your yellow hat, and your fake-fur earmuffs,
and two pairs of striped mittens,
one on top of the other."

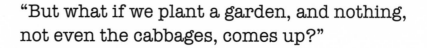

"But what if we plant a garden, and nothing, not even the cabbages, comes up?"

"We go to the nursery
and buy seven tomato plants, just in case.
When we come home, we dig seven holes in the garden
and put a tomato plant and compost in each one.
We pat the earth back around each tomato plant
and pour a bucket of water around each one, too,
to make them feel at home.

"Then we go inside to read a book.
When we come out again, there is a tiny row
of cabbage seedlings, and also
the bush beans have come up."

"But what if a bee stings me?"

"You run to the kitchen,
and I rub a piece of raw onion
back and forth and back and forth
on the sting.
You say:
A piece of onion? That is silly!
That won't work!
But it does."

"But what if I am mad at everyone?"

"You run away.
You pack raisins, walnuts,
oranges, crackers, and a flashlight
in a red bandanna.

"You knot its four corners together,
and tie it to a stick,
and carry it over your shoulder.

"You walk and walk till you come to the park.
You stay all afternoon, sitting by yourself
under a tree, and then on a bench.
Then you swing, pushing yourself off so hard
you go up so high you make up a song to yourself
about being a bird.
When you come home again,
you are not mad at everyone."

"But what if someone doesn't like me?"

"You feel lonely and sad.
You walk and walk until you come to a small pond.
You kneel in the grass by the edge of this pond,
and you see something move.
You put out your hand, and a tiny frog,
no bigger than your thumbnail, hops into it.
Very carefully, you lift your hand up to your ear,
and the frog whispers:
Other people like you. Other people love you.
Maybe that person will like you again, maybe not.
In any case, you're likable, and lovable, and it is all right.
Because a frog tells you this, you believe it."

"But what if I forget my lines in the school play?"

"You make up new ones, then and there.
And later, everyone will say:

What a wise and sensible child!
She forgot her lines, so she made up new ones!"

"But what if nobody likes the way I dance?"

"You go dancing in the woods,
alone in the crackling leaves.
One day you meet someone else,
dancing in the leaves.

"You dance together.
You throw leaves on each other.
You gather leaves into a big pile,
and jump into them.

"Then you go home and draw pictures
and drink cocoa with whipped cream."

"My loving doesn't die.
It stays with you,
as warm as two pairs of mittens, one pair on top of the other.
When you remember you and me, you say:
What can I do with so much love?
I will have to give some away."

"So you love thunder and lightning,
snow, planting cabbages, and bees.

"You dance with other people in the leaves,
and are in plays with them, and run away with them,
and read books with them, and get mad at them,
and make up with them.
You love them, and they love you,
and you eat raisins together."

"So it will be okay?"

"Yes, my love, it will.
It will be okay."